Frozen

Frozen

LORI JAMISON

HIP Xtreme Novels

NATIONAL LIBRARY OF CANADA CATALOGUING IN PUBLICATION DATA
Jamison, Lori, 1955–
        Frozen / Lori Jamison.

ISBN 978-1-926847-31-3

        I. Title.

PS8619.A67F76 2012   jC813'.6   C2012-901226-2

General editor: Paul Kropp
Text Design: Laura Brady
Illustrations by: Charlie Hnatiuk
Cover design: Robert Corrigan

1 2 3 4 5 6 7   17 16 15 14 13 12

Printed and bound in Canada

High Interest Publishing acknowledges the financial support of the
Government of Canada through the Canada Book Fund for our
publishing activities.

It was cold. So cold I couldn't really feel it anymore. I just felt tired. I wanted to lie down and rest. I wanted to give up the struggle.

I was ready to die.

Why keep fighting? I asked myself. *You're out here alone. In the Arctic, freezing, all by yourself. Your best buddy is dead. And maybe you should be dead too.*

Stop it. That was another voice in my head. *Things are bad, but they're not over. It's not over until the fat lady sings.*

My dad used to say that. It's not over until the fat lady sings. What did that mean? Who was the fat lady? Why didn't I ever ask him that?

But maybe when I die, maybe then I can ask him. Some people think so. Maybe there is a heaven and maybe I'll get there. I just have to let myself go. . . .

Contents

Chapter 1

Going Along

The first rule of survival is simple – be prepared.

That means having a plan. And sticking to the plan. And having a backup plan in case the first plan doesn't work.

It means having warm clothes and matches and water that isn't frozen. It means having some food and a GPS or a compass. It means . . . not being stupid.

But we were stupid.

It started when Frank came by on a snowmobile. We live in a small town near the Arctic Circle. The only way to get around is by snowmobile or by truck or by foot, so most of us use a snowmobile when we can. My dad has three of them. On any given day, maybe two of them work.

But Frank's mom didn't have a snowmobile. That's what surprised me when Frank showed up on one. He left the snowmobile running when he pounded on my door.

"Hey, Ray, get out of bed. Let's go. Let's blow this town."

I pushed away all the boots by the door and opened it.

"I'm not in bed, Frank. It's ten in the morning," I told him.

Have I mentioned that Frank is a bit crazy? He's always pushing me to do stuff and try things. He's the guy who plays out on the ice floes during the spring melt. He's the guy who kicks at Snarly Joe's dogs. He's the guy who gets in trouble.

Not me. I'm the good kid. I'm the kid who always plays by the rules. The one who can be trusted. The one who does well at school.

Still, Frank and I are friends. We've been friends since I moved up here, five years ago. Frank taught me how to deal with the winter cold and the summer mud. He taught me which guys would thump me and which guys didn't matter. Frank had "street smarts," as

we used to say in the city.

Frank's got a mess of black hair and a crazy look in his eyes. I've got light brown hair and pale blue eyes. My skin is so pale it looks like a sheet of paper.

Frank looks like he belongs up here. Maybe he does. He's half Inuit and looks it. I look like some kid from down south. Hey, I *am* a kid from down south. A real *kabloona*, as the local guys say.

"Where'd you get the Ski-doo?" I asked him.

"My uncle," he replied. Frank has about ten uncles here.

"He said you could use it?"

"Yeah, kind of." Frank gave me a grin, so I knew he was lying. "Anyhow, he'll never know."

"Never know what?"

"That you and I are doing a little hunting and fishing."

"We are?" I said.

"Yeah. It's good for you. Learn to live like a Northern guy. Get that chip off your shoulder."

Frank said that a lot. So I looked at my shoulder, then gave Frank a nasty look.

"Okay, so maybe you don't have a chip on your shoulder. But we've got a chance to get out of town, back to the land. Do some fishing. Some hunting."

"Where?" I asked.

"About an hour out of town – beside the river. I heard my uncle talking about caribou. I know he goes fishing out there."

Frank's uncle was Inuit. He knew how to hunt and fish. He could shoot a caribou and have food for the winter. Or catch a few fish and have a greasy feast for days. I'd eaten all that food at Frank's house.

My family wasn't like that. We got our food once a year, when the boat brought our supplies from down south. Anything else we got from the Northern store. And that was always expensive.

"C'mon, Ray. We've only got about six hours of light left. We've gotta get a move on. Don't be a wuss."

"Okay. Let me just tell my ma. . . ."

"Whoa!" Frank said, grabbing my arm. "Don't start telling her about this. She'll tell my mom and my mom will tell my uncle and. . . ."

"I thought you said your uncle was okay with this," I shot back.

"Kind of okay," Frank replied. "Listen – we'll be back long before dark. Nobody has to know. If we get a caribou or a few fish, then I'm a hero. If not, I've got a real big candy bar. And then we don't have to explain to nobody."

"Anybody," I said, correcting him. "We won't have to explain to anybody."

He shot me a look. "Whatever!"

"Okay," I said. "I'll tell her I'm going to your place." That was a small lie – a white lie. White like the snow out there.

"Six hours," Frank said. "Trust me."

"Yeah, I trust you," I said as I ducked into the house.

That was the second stupid thing I said. The first one was "okay" and going along on this trip. I didn't have a plan and, as it turned out, Frank didn't have much of a plan either. What's worse, neither of us had a backup plan.

Chapter 2

Breakdown

I got on the back of the Ski-doo and pulled my hood around my face. It was cold that day. In March, it gets down well below freezing in this part of the Southern Arctic. That's nothing. In the winter, we hit –40 or –70 with the wind chill. But this was almost spring and it wasn't that cold. At least, not cold until the wind blew into your face.

Frank's uncle had a pretty nice Ski-doo. There was plenty of room for both of us. Frank got in front and revved the motor. I climbed behind him and grabbed the handles at the rear. Then the Ski-doo took off.

I said that Frank was crazy. Maybe that's why he drove the Ski-doo so fast. I could feel the back rest pressed into me as we zoomed forward.

"You in a hurry?" I shouted. But Frank couldn't hear me. The snowmobile was making a wild roar. The town around us was a blur.

And then we were out on the land. Around us was the white of the barrens. We'd had snow last week, so the land was still white and pure. That's one great thing about the Arctic – the white, white snow. Back in the city, snow turns to slush and gets black with dirt. Out here, the snow always stays white. White and clean.

After a half hour, Frank slowed the Ski-doo to a stop.

"Are we here?" I asked him.

"Not yet," he told me. "We've got to follow the river, maybe another half an hour."

"I'm already cold," I said.

"Don't be a *wuss*," he snapped. "We'll make a fire when we get there."

Then the Ski-doo roared forward. We were heading farther into the land. We'd soon be a long way from town, a long way from the shore of Hudson's Bay. And all around us was . . . nothing. Just white snow stretching as far as I could see.

On a sunny day, the snow could be beautiful. But today there were gray clouds overhead. In the distance, there were bigger clouds – storm clouds.

I tapped Frank on the shoulder. He slowed the Skidoo and leaned back.

"You check the weather?" I shouted.

"It's cold," he shouted to me. "But we'll be back soon."

"I just meant. . . ." but I couldn't finish. We were roaring ahead.

Snow. They say the Inuit have a hundred names for snow. White show, hard snow, soft snow, snow to make igloos, wet snow . . . kinds of snow we don't have in the south. It's beautiful stuff, all white and clean. But it's also a bit scary. It's cold and icy. It can be slippery or get you wet. It can cover over cracks in the ice. Snow can hide problems unless you can see past it.

And problems up here can get very bad, very quickly.

We were racing along, moving fast, when I heard a funny noise. Then I could smell something – it was like burning rubber. I tapped Frank on the shoulder, but he was already slowing down.

When we stopped, we could both see smoke coming from the motor.

Frank swore. I shook my head.

"What is it?" I asked him.

"The drive belt," Frank replied, swearing again. "My uncle just changed the belt. But maybe. . . ."

Frank lifted the plastic shell of the snowmobile. Now we could see below to the engine and the track. There was the drive belt, still smoking.

Frank swore again.

"So what now?" I asked.

"Look at this," he said, pointing to the belt. "It's shot. The rubber is melted. The metal is just wrapped around. It's — "

"Is there another belt?"

"Well, I don't know. But it's not a bad idea to look around," Frank replied. He opened a cover at the back of the Ski-doo. "Yeah, here we go. Another belt. Looks like my uncle was planning ahead."

More than we could say for ourselves, I thought. But I didn't say anything.

"Trouble is. . . ." Frank told me as he looked down, "we've got to get the old belt off. And then get this one on. Easy to do in a shop, but out here?"

I looked around. Out here was empty snow in every direction. The wind was blowing harder. The dark clouds in the distance were coming closer.

"Is there a tool kit?" I asked.

"Should be," Frank replied. Then he began looking around inside the compartment. "But it's not here. Any chance you've got a knife?" He looked at me and I stared back.

"Yeah, right. I had a lot of time to bring a knife and

a tool kit and all that," I told him.

"I'm just asking."

"And I'm just telling you."

So it was kind of tense for a second or two. Then Frank went back to the motor and tried to pull the old belt off. He was having a hard time. The drive belt had melted on pretty tight. If we had a knife, we could cut it. But we didn't have a knife.

After a couple of minutes, Frank looked up. "I got an idea. How about I shoot it?"

"With what?" I asked.

"I brought a rifle. I could. . . ."

"You could shoot your hand off," I told him. "You're crazy. You need a knife and a screwdriver and a wrench."

"Yeah, yeah," Frank sighed. "How come you're always so smart, Ray? How come I've always got to be the stupid guy?"

"I didn't say that," I told him. That was the truth. I didn't even *think* that. "We just had some bad luck."

"Yeah, a lot of bad luck," Frank told me. "This thing is toast," he said, pointing to the dead Ski-doo. "We're an hour from town and it's going to be dark in three hours. We could be stuck out here all night. Did

I miss anything?"

"Yeah, the weather. The clouds over there aren't looking good." The dark clouds were coming toward us pretty fast.

Frank said nothing. He slumped against the back of the snowmobile. I stood there feeling helpless.

"Maybe somebody will come out this way," I said. "Your uncle said there was good fishing and hunting."

If we were stuck like this down south, we'd use a cell phone. But cell phones don't work up here. You've got to use a satellite phone, and they cost a lot. Too much for us. Down south, we could expect somebody to come along. Some other hunter would show up, or some kids on snowmobiles. But up here? There were no roads. Sometimes there was a snowmobile path, but we couldn't see one. We were in the middle of nowhere, and we had nothing.

Then the first snow began to fall.

"I don't like this, Frank," I said.

"You think I do?" he snapped back. "We could get real cold if nobody finds us."

But nobody – nobody – knew where we were.

Chapter 3

Digging In

Down south, people think it snows a lot in the Arctic. That's not true. In many ways, the Arctic is very dry. More snow falls in Chicago or Montreal than we get up here. But in the Arctic the snow doesn't melt until the summer. So we really have two seasons here – winter and mud.

But sometimes – sometimes – we get a blizzard. The Inuit have a name for it: *piqiq*.

I've been in blizzards down south, and they can be nasty. Snow clogs the streets, highways close down, cars go sliding. But up here, a blizzard can be deadly. Suddenly there's snow, lots of it. But the wind and cold make it worse. We can hit –70 in a blizzard, even worse when the wind blows. It's so bad you can get frostbite in a minute or less. You can get lost and freeze to death in no time at all.

That doesn't happen down south. But it really does happen here. Frank and I were afraid it could happen to us.

"What time is it?" Frank asked me.

"Two o'clock."

"So we've got four hours or so until sundown."

"Yeah." The sun stays down all winter, but by March we had almost ten hours of daylight.

"Four hours for somebody to find us." Frank was really talking to himself, but I heard him.

"Yeah, somebody who's dumb enough to go out into a snowstorm," I said. "Any chance your uncle might come back? If he sees that his snowmobile is gone, he might come looking."

Frank shook his head. "He flew to Iqaluit."

"You tell anybody we were coming out here?"

Frank just gave me a look. Of course not.

So there we were, out on the land. It was well below freezing and a storm was coming up. We had – at most – three hours to do something. That didn't leave much time to come up with a plan.

"You got any ideas?" I asked him.

"Yeah," he said. "We go to the first rule of survival."

"What's that?"

"Don't panic."

"Okay, I'm not panicking. I'm not scared. Now what's the second rule?" I asked him.

"Don't pee your pants," he told me.

"Really?"

"Nah, that's the same as the first rule. The second rule is to find shelter," Frank said.

I looked around us. There was nothing but snow, mostly flat snow and ice.

"Or *make* shelter," Frank went on. "See that ridge of snow over there? We can dig into it and make a cave for the night. It won't be great, but it'll keep us alive."

"Dig with what?" I asked him. "We didn't bring anything."

"Yes we did. I've got fishing line and a gun," he said. "And we've got the Ski-doo. My uncle will kill me, but we'll have to take it apart."

"There's no tool kit."

"Yeah, but we've got muscle," Frank said. "See the snow flap back there? It's just held on with a couple of bolts. One little pull. . . ."

It took more than one little pull. Both of us had to yank on the snow flap, then we finally got it free. That gave us a little piece of hard rubber to use, not even two feet by two feet square.

But a little piece of rubber was better than nothing.

"We're going to make ourselves a cave," Frank told me. "Then we can sleep tight, just like bears in the winter."

Frank got started first. He began digging into the

ridge of snow. He used the flap like a scoop, pulling away snow. He kept digging halfway between the bottom and the top of the ridge. I kicked away the snow as he dug.

But ten minutes was all he could take. "Your turn," he said.

He hadn't made much of an indent in the snow. The "cave" was maybe a foot into the ridge. Not much shelter for two guys in a storm. But I kept working at it. There was nothing else we could do.

We had only one bit of good luck – the snow wasn't packed. The Ski-doo snow flap was a lousy shovel, but it was good enough with the snow we had.

I kept digging for ten minutes, but I didn't make it as far as Frank.

"We're getting there," he said, taking over.

"Barely," I said.

"Don't talk like that, Ray. You gotta stay positive."

"Yeah, like I'm real positive right now."

Frank grunted and kept digging into the snow ridge. Soon he had made a cave big enough that one guy could fit inside it.

"Getting there," he said, handing me the flap.

"Yeah, but the snow is starting," I told him.

"Think positive, Ray. And dig," he said.

It wasn't just snow that was the problem. The wind made it worse. As I dug into the ridge, the wind blew snow into my face. The snow got inside my coat and then began to melt against my skin. *Nice*, I thought, *real nice.*

I handed the snow flap back to Frank. He did a better job digging than I did. I guess he was stronger. Or maybe he knew just how bad things were going to get.

I kept hoping that somebody would find us. When I wasn't digging, I'd look off onto the flat land. I kept hoping that somebody would come racing out.

But nobody came.

It was just us. Two guys trying to dig a snow cave. Two guys with a broken snowmobile now half-buried under the snow.

And it was getting dark.

I looked at my watch. A little after four o'clock. Sundown in March would be a little past six o'clock. The night would be fourteen hours long.

"We're just about there," Frank told me. "A nice, cozy cave . . . for two. It's not the Super 8 motel, but it's what we've got."

So that was our cave. A hole in the side of a snow ridge, maybe four feet deep. It was about as wide and tall as we were, so it would be a tight fit.

"We're going to sleep in that?" I asked him.

"Yeah. Just like an igloo, kind of," Frank said. "Now we just have to close ourselves inside. You get in there, Ray. I'll throw in some plastic sheets and the stuff I brought. Then I'll build up the outside wall."

So I crawled into our snow cave, then pushed myself against the back wall. The snow was cold, but not as cold as the wind outside.

Frank threw in a few plastic bags from the snowmobile. Then his kit with the fishing gear and the gun. At last, he began building up snow at the opening to our cave. He built a wall maybe three feet high, then stepped over it to get inside. Then he began piling up more snow.

"You going to wall us in?" I asked him.

"Mostly," he said. "If it works, this becomes our door." He held up the snow flap. "And then we just settle down. You bring any cards?"

"Yeah, right," I told him.

"Then it's going to be a long, boring night."

Chapter 4

The First Night

"You scared of the dark?" Frank asked.

"No," I told him.

"Me neither," he said. But I think he was lying. I know I was lying.

I was afraid of the dark and the cold and the blizzard outside. I was scared that nobody would find us. Nobody would ever find us. I was afraid I'd freeze in the night. I was afraid the morning would never come.

My brain kept racing. Freezing. Coughing. Wolves. Polar bears. There are a lot of ways to die in the Arctic. None of them are good ones.

At first, there was a little light from around our

snow flap door. Then the night outside grew black. Our little cave got even blacker. With the darkness came the cold. I know for a fact that it was no colder then than it was before. But it *felt* colder. I was sitting in the dark, my butt on a plastic bag, my back against a wall of snow. I could *feel* the cold all around me. I could breathe it. I could feel it come through my coat, freezing my back. But my fingers were the worst. That's where the frostbite gets you first – in the fingers. Even under my gloves, I could feel my fingers getting colder and colder.

"Hey, I've got a little good news," Frank said.

"Could use some of that."

"Hand me that plastic bag."

He could have gotten the bag himself, but I did what he said. I pushed the bag up to him and Frank reached around inside.

"You going fishing?" I asked.

"Not a bad joke," he replied. "Got any more?"

"Knock knock."

"Who's there?"

"Snow," I said.

"Snow who?"

"Snow business like show business," I said. "Get it?"

Frank shook his head. We were so close I could feel the air move. "What is that? A kindergarten joke?"

"Yeah, pretty much."

"Right," Frank mumbled. He was playing around with something, but I couldn't see in the dark. "Now the matches . . ." he said, talking to himself.

Then there was a *pffft* and a bright spot of light. Frank had lit a match. In the dim light, I saw something on the floor in front of him. Then the match went out.

Frank swore.

"Waterproof matches?" I asked.

"I wish," he replied. "Kitchen matches. I've got two packs."

Two packs. How many matches are in two packs? Forty, maybe. If the packs were fresh. If they were like matches from my house, there might be all of ten decent matches left.

Pfft. Frank lit another one. It didn't even light up. *Pfft*, a third match. Now the whole cave smelled like sulfur.

"You think maybe. . . ."

"Shut up and watch," he snapped at me. "Secret native lore, Ray. You guys can learn from us." Frank is half Inuit. Sometimes he reminds me of it. Then he

tells me I'm just a stupid white guy from the south.

Pfft, the match lit and stayed lit. Frank lowered it slowly, then touched it to something.

"What's that?" I asked him.

"A *kudlik*," he told me. "Or an oil lamp in simple English. You said you were afraid of the dark, right?"

"No I didn't," I shot back.

"Never mind. This little baby will keep us toasty warm all night," he said.

"Toasty warm?"

"Okay, a little bit warm. Better than freezing our butts off. We could have played cards if you brought any."

"Yeah, so what do we do now?" I asked him.

"You got any better jokes?"

I didn't have any better jokes, at least not right away. Frank tried to remember more knock-knock jokes. Then we made up some really stupid ones. Then I tried a couple of jokes my dad always tells. So we didn't get to the dirty jokes for half an hour.

An hour after that, we were all out of jokes. We tried to sing a couple of songs, but neither of us can hold a tune. We couldn't remember the words either. So then we tried to tell stories. That's what the Inuit used to do. In the long winter nights, they'd sing songs and tell stories. But I think they were better at it than Frank and I were.

Around eight, I got hungry.

"You got any food in that kit?" I asked.

"Nope," Frank told me. "We were going to catch fish, remember? Or shoot something. I didn't figure we'd need a can of beans."

"What about that candy bar?"

Frank didn't say anything. He just reached into his pocket and gave me the empty wrapper.

"What's this?" I asked Frank. I added a couple of swear words, just because.

"All that's left," he told me. "I got a little hungry."

I could feel the blood pouring into my face. "But you said we were going to save it. Just in case. You remember that?"

"Yeah, but I got hungry," Frank said. "I was digging pretty hard."

"Well, so was I."

"It was in *my* pocket," he said. "I brought it. You brought exactly nothing."

I didn't say a thing. I was too angry.

After five minutes of silence, Frank figured out

how I felt.

"Sorry, buddy," he said in a small voice. "I guess I was kind of stupid. I wasn't thinking."

"Your stomach was thinking," I told him.

"Yeah, but my stomach isn't real smart," he said.

We both laughed. It was going to be a long night. There was no sense getting mad at each other. We had to get along. That's one of the rules of survival – get along. Even if you want to beat up the other guy, you've got to get along.

Outside, we could hear the wind howling. It blew in around our "door" and made the *kudlik* fire dance at our feet. It also blew smoke around the top of our cave.

Frank read my mind. He reached into his kit and pulled out his fishing rod. In a second, he'd pushed a hole through the "roof" of our cave.

"To help you breathe," he said.

"Thanks," I replied. The air inside our cave got a little better. But it also got a lot colder. If I'd had a blanket, I would have curled up inside it. But all I had was Frank.

"You ready to sleep?" he asked me. I pushed up beside him. He smelled like grease.

"Yeah, I guess."

"Sweet dreams," he added.

In ten minutes, Frank was snoring. It took me a lot longer to get to sleep. I kept thinking about all the stupid mistakes we'd made. I kept wondering about the next day. Would anybody find us?

At last I was able to get to sleep. And I had plenty of dreams that night, but none of them were sweet.

Chapter 5

Morning Light

I woke up at six o'clock. I was confused at first. Where was I? Why was it so dark? It took a second or two to remember.

I was in a cave, a cave we had dug in the snow. There had been a blizzard. We had crawled inside and Frank was right in front of me. He was still asleep, snoring.

Last night we had a lamp, a *kudlik*, that gave some light. But this morning, it was coal black in our cave. The *kudlik* must have run out of oil. Or maybe one of us had knocked it over during the night.

My body felt stiff, as if it were frozen. But I wasn't frozen – not yet. I was just cold. The cold outside seemed to have gotten into my bones.

I tried to move, but I felt so stiff. There was a pain in my lower back and my right leg. And Frank was like a dead weight in front of me. So what was the point of moving. There was nowhere to go. The sun wouldn't come up for two more hours.

Two hours. Two hours before anyone would even start to look for us.

I closed my eyes and tried to go back to sleep. Maybe I did. Maybe not. But a while later, I could feel Frank's head moving.

"Ray, you awake?" he asked.

"I am now."

"What time is it?"

"Give me a second." I had a hard time lifting my arm. Then I had to push the button on my watch to see the time. All this meant shifting both of us around. "Six thirty," I told him.

"Almost sunrise."

"Well, in an hour and a bit."

"No sense punching our way out of here," Frank said. "It'll be a lot colder outside."

"Can you light the lamp again?"

Frank shook his head. I could feel it; I couldn't see

it. "No more oil. I only brought enough oil for a few hours."

"Too bad."

"Yeah," Frank said, pausing a moment. "You know, I was having a dream when I woke up. I was dreaming about Mexico. I was lying on the beach and the sun was way up in the sky and it was hot. Way hot, man."

"Nice dream," I told him. I had been having a dream too. I dreamed I was buried alive under the snow. I was buried and slowly freezing to death. I liked Frank's dream a lot better.

"You ever been to Mexico?" he asked me.

"Nope. I don't speak Spanish."

"Ah, they all speak English down there. At least at the resorts. You lie on the beach and guys come and bring you drinks. The sun beats down, you get hot and your skin gets brown. It's nice, man. Real nice. I'm going back there someday."

"Tell me about it," I said.

So Frank did – and maybe it seems weird, but it passed the time. He talked all about sunshine and sunscreen and Mexican food. Then I talked about Florida and Disneyland. And then it was eight o'clock. Sunrise.

But we couldn't see any sun. Our snow flap must have been all sealed in by blowing snow.

"Okay, buddy. It's time to rise and shine," Frank said. "Get your sunglasses ready. You don't want to go blind when we step outside."

Frank was right. If the sun was shining, we could go snow-blind in seconds.

If we could have seen ourselves, we would have looked funny. Two guys in pitch darkness with sunglasses – like the Blues Brothers. But inside a cave.

"Okay, I'm going to kick at the snow flap," Frank told me.

He leaned back into me so his legs went up. Then he gave a kick at the snowmobile flap that was our "door." He kicked once, twice. I expected to see some light come in from the edges. Or maybe the flap would go flying out. But nothing happened.

"Must have been a big storm last night," Frank said.

"Yeah," I replied. I tried my best to sound cool and in control. But I was scared. What if we were buried under the snow? What if there was no way out of our cave?

But I didn't panic. Not that morning. I stayed cool

and even had a good idea.

"You get beside me and we'll both push," I told Frank.

"Yeah, that's good. Ready . . . on the count of three."

On *three*, we pushed the snow flap out and away. Suddenly there was light and snow and cold, cold air – all coming into our cave. It made me grateful for the dark and the warmth of the *kudlik*. Now we had the real Arctic to deal with.

We climbed out of our cave, and everything was white. The sun was hazy and low down, but the white of everything was almost too much to bear.

"Big storm," Frank said. "We were really buried in there."

"Where's the snowmobile?"

"It's . . . uh. . . . "

We both looked around the flat white land. Perfect new snow everywhere. No tracks. No sign that anything – human or not – had ever been here.

"Okay, so remember," I said. "Think back."

"It was this way," Frank told me, walking in one direction. "I bet I'll step on the thing."

But he was wrong. It took ten minutes of searching to find the snowmobile. It was buried under two feet of snow. That was one big storm, even for the Arctic.

So we took the snow flap and dug like crazy. In a few minutes, the yellow of the snowmobile was bright against the snow.

"Okay, now the planes can see us," Frank said.

"The planes," I repeated.

"Search and rescue," Frank said. He spoke like this happened all the time. "Your mom will have called, and they send out planes."

"Yeah, but my mom thinks I'm at your house," I said.

"Well, then, my dad would call. They'll look in my bed and see I'm not there, so they'll call around. Maybe call your place first. They'll see that the snowmobile is gone. Then they'll figure out that we're out here. Simple as that."

"Simple," I agreed.

"In the meanwhile, we just hang out."

"We try not to freeze," I said. The cold was already freezing my fingers.

"Maybe we do some hunting," Frank said. He acted like this was nothing more than a winter camping trip.

"Yeah, right. But first I've got a little problem."

"Me too," Frank agreed.

It's hard to make zippers work when your fingers are really cold. The zippers get stuck, the snow pants don't open up right. And then you've got to aim so the pee doesn't go down your leg. It's not easy, but you can do it.

"Oooh, that feels better," Frank said.

Steam came up from the pee, and then it froze in seconds on top of the snow.

"Now we just wait for search and rescue," Frank said. "No problem at all."

Chapter 6

Up There, Look!

No problem at all, I said to myself. The sky was clear over our heads. Someone in a plane could see for miles. Someone coming on a snowmobile could see for miles.

Of course, that someone would have to be looking.

Was anybody looking? Did anybody have a clue where we were?

I guessed we'd come thirty miles – make that about 50 km – from town. But what direction? Frank said he was looking for a place by a river. But any river was frozen now, and covered with snow. Frank's uncle knew the place, but he had gone on a trip down south. Had he told anybody else?

So I tried to do some math in my head. Let's say a search plane goes flying. It goes about 200 km an hour, but it has to fly back and forth in a grid. Suppose the grid is 50 km. So the plane can do four runs on the grid in an hour. How far can a pilot see from a small plane? Maybe 5 km on each side. So if the plane does four passes, 10 km apart, it'll look over 40 km in an hour. So it'll fly over a 50 km square in just over an hour.

Not bad, I said to myself. If my math was right, we'd be rescued before noon. By lunchtime, we'd be home and getting chewed out by our parents. I'd be grounded for a month. Frank would be . . . well, who knows? After the damage to his uncle's Ski-doo, he could be grounded for years.

I wasn't looking forward to that part. My parents would be looking at me. They'd use their line: "We're not angry; we're disappointed." Then they'd get the *disappointed* look. And I'd feel stupid and ashamed. But still, I'd get some lunch.

A little food would be a very good thing, I said to myself.

"You say something?" Frank asked.

"No, but I was doing some math. I think we'll be

rescued by noon," I said.

"If they see us," Frank replied.

"Yeah, well, they can see the snowmobile. And we'll be waving at the plane," I said.

"A snowmobile is pretty small if they're flying at 2000 feet. So are we," Frank said. "They might not see us on the first pass."

"I thought you told me to be positive," I snapped at him. I guess I was hungry. Frank was getting on my nerves.

"Yeah, but you've got to be real, too. A little smoke would sure help them find us," he said. "I was thinking of getting some gas from the Ski-doo. Then maybe we burn something that'll make a lot of smoke."

"Like the snowmobile seat," I said.

"Yeah, that would work," he said. "But my uncle would kill me. So maybe just the snow flap. That could be enough. Meanwhile, you flash a mirror at the plane."

"What mirror?"

"Oh, I forgot," Frank said. "So maybe flash with your watch. Something like that."

Frank went to get some gas from the Ski-doo. And I started thinking. I thought about what we needed to survive. The basic kit. The kind of kit anybody with half a brain would have brought with them. A blanket. A mirror. Waterproof matches. A flare. A compass. A map. Water. Food.

I wasn't even thinking about a satellite phone. That would be too much. But we didn't even have a mirror. And Frank had eaten the only candy bar.

What did we have? Some soggy matches, some pieces of snowmobile, some plastic bags. We wouldn't last a week in a forest down south. But here we were, in the Arctic, trying to get by with nothing. It was all so stupid, and it made me mad.

"Hey, Ray," Frank shouted.

"What?" I shot back at him. I was angry and didn't want to talk.

"Up there, in the sky. Look."

I turned to look where Frank pointed. There was something dark in the sky. It could have been a bird, or a flock of birds. It could have been a plane. It could have been a speck on my sunglasses. So we waited.

The speck got bigger, getting closer to us.

"I think it's a plane," Frank said.

I still wasn't sure, but the plane/bird was flying straight at us. In a couple of seconds, I could see that it *was* a plane. It was coming from town, flying in our direction.

"Okay, we gotta move," Frank said.

He had filled a cup with gasoline from the Ski-doo. Now he poured it on the snow flap and reached in his pocket for matches.

Pfft. Nothing.

"What do I do?" I asked him.

"Start waving. Move around. Try to look like a person and not a caribou!"

I could do that. I grabbed a couple of plastic bags and began waving with them. Then I went running to the Ski-doo and over to our cave, then back again. As the plane got really close, I started to shout.

"Hey, we're down here. Down here!" I screamed. It was stupid, I knew. Nobody could hear me. I was wasting my body heat and my lung power. But still I screamed. "Down here! You're looking for us!"

All the while, I kept looking over at Frank. He'd gone through five matches now, and only one had caught. It didn't stay lit long enough to light the gasoline.

"Sh— " Frank swore. He kept on swearing. In no time, he went through three more matches. It was

getting stupid. We might need those matches.

"Give it up," I shouted to him. "You wave, too. I'll flash my watch."

So Frank did. He put the matches back in his pocket, then began to run back and forth. I got over by our cave and tried to signal the plane by bouncing sunlight off my watch. But that was crazy. I was flashing at the whole sky, not the plane.

"We're here!" Frank shouted. Now he was as stupid

as me. "Down here."

The plane was almost right over us.

"Help us!" we screamed. We were both running around like crazy, waving like crazy.

And the plane kept flying.

"Did they see us?" I asked Frank. I was out of breath. I could feel the cold air biting my lungs. "Do you think?"

"Maybe," Frank coughed. He was out of breath too. "But it wasn't search and rescue."

"How do you know?"

"Wrong plane," Frank told me. He was breathing hard. "It was a regular flight. Maybe the noon flight to Iqaluit."

"Still, they must have seen us," I said.

"Yeah, they must have."

"We were making enough noise," I said.

"Yeah, right," Frank replied. "That was kind of a waste."

"Yeah," I admitted. "Kind of stupid."

The plane had disappeared. Now there was only the hazy sky – a hazy sky with a few clouds.

"They saw us, right?" I asked Frank. I knew he didn't have an answer, but I had to ask.

"Yeah, they had to," he said. "Keep an eye out for snowmobiles. Somebody will be out to get us right away."

"Right away," I repeated. My lungs hurt and my eyes were wet with tears. "Right away," I said one more time.

Chapter 7
Waiting

Let me tell you about cold. Down south, in the cities, people don't know cold. All they know is snow and slush. They know wind whipping between buildings. They know a kind of damp chill. Those city people go into Starbucks, have a cup of coffee, and forget about the cold. It's nothing. Cold is just something you feel while you wait for the bus. The warm bus.

But there are other kinds of cold. There's wilderness cold. That's when you go out camping or hunting or hiking in the winter. Wilderness cold can be pretty mean. But if you dress for it – layers of clothes and a good parka – it's not awful. You feel the cold on your face sometimes. You feel it work into your boots sometimes. But it's no big deal. Because there's a tent or a cabin or a fire. You can get away from the cold and warm up.

Then there's Arctic cold. It's always mean and sometimes deadly. On a good, sunny day it will chill your skin in a few minutes. If you forget your gloves, you've got to watch for frostbite. And that's on a good day. On a bad day the temperature gets to −40 or below and the wind blows like crazy. Any exposed skin freezes fast – sometimes in seconds. A wet finger will stick to metal instantly. Frostbite can begin in seconds. In a few minutes, your whole finger can freeze through. Then the skin and muscles are all dead. There's nothing a doctor can do but cut it off. Lots of guys up here are missing a finger or two . . . because of the cold.

The cold. Out there, all around you, waiting for one mistake.

"So where's the —ing plane?" Frank asked me again.

Frank was swearing more now. It was one o'clock and we hadn't seen another plane. No snowmobiles. Nothing. We had five hours until sundown and a second night. But this second night we wouldn't have

a *kudlik*. We'd only have each other.

"I think the cold is getting to you," I said.

"I think hunger is getting to me. And cold. And everything," he said. Frank turned to me with a funny look on his face. "You know what, Ray? This isn't fun anymore. I stopped having fun about two hours ago."

"Me too," I said.

We fell into silence.

If the first plane had seen us, they'd have sent help. We'd be rescued by now. So our only hope was a second plane – a search and rescue plane. But there were no planes. Nothing flew across the sky but birds.

I wondered if anyone knew we were missing. Was there anything on local radio? Were the cops checking houses in town? Did anybody care?

No, that wasn't fair. I knew my mom really cared about me. Frank's mom and dad, they cared about him. It's not like we were orphans up here. But the search people must be going the wrong way. Maybe they were searching east or south, not northwest. Maybe they had just missed us. Maybe they were real close, even now.

But the sky wasn't looking good. Dark clouds were coming up. There might be another storm, and that would ground the rescue planes. We were going to have one more night out on these barren lands, that was for sure. Somehow we had to make it through.

"I've got an idea," I said to Frank.

"That's a first," he snapped back.

I ignored him. "How about we start up the Ski-doo? There's still a lot of gas. The engine will get warm and then we can get warm along with it."

"Not bad, Ray. We can even melt some of this snow and get a real drink of water." We'd been eating snow all morning, but that's not a good idea. It cools you down too much.

"Maybe make a cup of tea," I said. That was a bit silly, but it sounded good.

"Tea and biscuits," Frank went on. "Just like at the town hotel."

Except we didn't have any biscuits. And the water would never get hot enough to make tea. But the snowmobile did start up, and the engine did get warm.

Frank and I got on either side of the engine and kind of hugged it.

"This is kind of weird," Frank said, "hugging a snowmobile."

"I can think of better things to hug," I told him.

"Yeah, me too. But at least the Ski-doo doesn't tell you to get lost, she's already got a boyfriend."

I laughed. It was the first laugh that day. It was also the last one.

We switched sides and got our butts warm. Then I got the idea of warming up the plastic bags. We did that, then stuck them in our coats. The heat didn't last long, but it felt good. Then we put snow inside the plastic bags. That turned them into hot water bottles. Pretty nice.

We were so busy with the engine and the plastic bags that we didn't watch the sky. We should have. Up above, there were big clouds rolling in. The air was feeling a bit warmer – but wet. Another storm was coming.

"What time is it?"

"A little after four," I said.

"No rescue," Frank said. "No rescue today."

I didn't say a word. What would be the point?

"So we're back in the cave tonight," Frank said. "Now I've got an idea. The *kudlik* works with oil. What if I poured in some gas?"

"From the snowmobile?" I asked him. "It would flame up for maybe two seconds – if you're lucky. Or if you used a lot, it could blow up. Did you know a can of gas is equal to a couple sticks of dynamite?"

"Well, thank you, Mr. Science," Frank replied. "It was just an idea to stay warm."

"Bad idea."

"Guess so," Frank admitted. "But it's going to be a cold night."

"Cold and hungry."

"Cold and hungry and boring."

All of that was true. The night would be cold, hungry and boring. It would also be scary. It would be the first night when we asked the worst question. What if nobody came to rescue us? How long could we last?

Chapter 8

Can't Take It Anymore

We woke up the next morning at six. That was the good news – we woke up. We hadn't died during the night. We hadn't frozen in our cave. We hadn't become two bodies lost under the snow.

But that was the only good news.

"I can't take it anymore," Frank said.

He was behind me this time. We switched places in the middle of the night. The guy at the back gets a frozen back; the guy at the front gets a frozen chest and face. So we switched halfway. That morning, we were frozen on both sides.

"Me neither," I agreed. "We need a rescue."

"We've waited two days for a rescue," Frank said.

"Two days! Two f— days." His voice was cracking up. I could almost hear him crying.

"Hey, Frank," I said, trying to sound calm. "Don't start losing it. Remember what you told me? The first rule – don't panic."

"It's not f—— panic!" he yelled. "It's . . . it's just . . . just making sense."

Of course Frank wasn't making sense himself. I didn't know, then, what he was thinking. He wouldn't tell me for another hour.

"C'mon, let's get out of here," I said, pushing at the snow flap. It fell out easily this time. "Let's go start up the snowmobile and get warm. C'mon."

Frank was still grumbling when we got outside. There had been no new snow that night, no blizzard. The sun was almost up at seven-thirty. A rescue plane could start flying any time. We just had to be ready.

We walked over to the Ski-doo. We still had plastic bags around our boots and gloves. If anyone had seen us, we must have looked pretty silly. But there was no one to see us. I would have given my right arm for somebody to see us, silly or not.

Frank pushed the starter button. Nothing. He pushed it again. Nothing.

"——" he swore.

"Let me," I said. As if my push would be better than his. Nothing.

"Okay, open it up," Frank said.

We lifted the engine cover and looked inside. This was a pretty new Ski-doo. A lot of the engine was covered in plastic. Still, we could see the battery.

"Battery looks okay," I said. I jiggled the two cables and they felt fine.

"Hit it," Frank told me.

"Huh?"

"Hit it," he repeated. "Sometimes you can get some juice just by hitting the thing. Let me get the snow flap."

This seemed a little crazy to me. It was like my dad doing shop work. If something didn't work, he'd go get a bigger hammer. Of course, we didn't have a hammer. We didn't have any tools.

Frank came back with the snow flap and whacked the battery. He hit it three times, as hard as he could.

"Okay, now try it," he ordered.

I pushed the button. Nothing. Not even a grunt from the engine.

Frank smashed the battery one more time. Then

he cursed and sat back on the ground.

"Done. Frozen. Just like us."

I looked at him and tried to stay calm. "They'll find us today. They've got to."

"How do you know?" Frank shouted at me. "How can you be so — sure? We've been out here for two days, waiting. Waiting for nothing. You know what I think, Ray? I don't think they're looking. I don't think anybody is f— looking. Maybe something went wrong. Maybe nobody reported us missing. Maybe . . . I don't know what. But nobody's looking. There's no rescue plane looking for us. There's no rescue team coming out. We're just stuck out here, waiting to. . . ."

Frank's voice broke before the last word. But I knew the word – *die.* We were stuck out in the frozen Arctic waiting to die.

"We can't just give up," I said.

"I'm not talking about giving up. I'm talking about rescue. I'm tired of waiting around here for nothing. I say we leave here and start moving down the river."

"You can't do that," I told him. "Isn't that one of the rules when you get lost? You don't go moving around if you want people to find you."

"Yeah, and I say f— that rule." Frank was looking wild, now.

"Look, we've got a kind of camp here. There's a cave to sleep in. Some plastic sheets. Some gasoline in the Ski-doo, even if it won't start. We can handle another day or two."

"You can, Ray. Not me. I've had enough. I can't take another day of this."

"You're being stupid," I shot back.

"Don't call me f— stupid, city boy. What do you know about staying alive out here? Squat. That's what you know. You'd be dead now if it wasn't for me."

"That's why we've got to stick together, Frank."

"So come with me," he said. He took off his sunglasses and looked right at me. But I could see his eyes were crazy. Frank had lost it.

"No way," I said. "You don't have a compass. You don't have a map. You don't have decent boots or snowshoes. It's stupid, Frank."

"I told you not to say that." He was crazy mad now. I could see it. He got up on his feet and he was stomping around like a crazy guy.

"I'm just saying. . . ."

But Frank wasn't listening. He went over to our cave and grabbed his kit. Then he threw the plastic bags inside.

"You can't do this," I said. I got over beside him.

"I'm doing it."

"Frank," I said, reaching out to him. "This is crazy. You're tired and hungry and cold. It's getting to you. You're judgment is going."

"Don't f— talk to me about judgment, city boy. I'm out of here. Down the river. I'll send you a postcard when I get home."

"Frank!" I tried to block him, but Frank was stronger than me. He gave me one push that sent me flying backward.

Then he started walking toward the river. Frank seemed to grow smaller as he went into the barren land. Then he was just a black dot against the white snow.

Chapter 9

The River

So I stood there. I knew right away that everything was wrong.

We had done everything wrong.

We had come out here without telling people. We had come out without a plan. We had no emergency supplies. We had no food, no water, only a few lousy matches. We had no shelter, no compass, no map.

We were a disaster waiting to happen.

Now the disaster was happening. Frank had panicked. He'd lost his cool. Now he was stomping off on his own. And the two of us were separated. That cut our odds of survival a lot.

In two days, we'd both be dead. We'd die alone on

the frozen land . . . unless something happened. We needed a rescue. We needed help.

So I tried to weigh the odds in my mind. I had the snowmobile and its gas. I had a cave already dug in the snow. The day was warmer than before, almost up to the freezing mark. Under the sun I might even be able to warm up.

But my best friend was walking off, alone. He was trying to get to town, and the odds were lousy. Town was at least 30 miles – make that 50 km – down the river. A man can walk maybe 5 km. an hour over good land. But over fresh snow, watching for cracks in the ice below, it would be slower. Frank would need at least 15 hours to get to town. If he made it to town.

I was right when I said that Frank was stupid.

But I guess I was stupid, too. I grabbed the plastic bags and the snow flap, then I began to walk after him.

You're an idiot, I said to myself.

He's my best friend, I answered back.

You're just scared to be out here by yourself.

So? I told myself. *Nobody wants to die alone. Why should I be any different?*

I broke rules number one and two. I panicked. I didn't stay put. But I made all sorts of excuses in my head. No one had found us in two days, after all. If we got closer to town, the chance of rescue would go up. The day was warm and we'd have a full eight hours to walk. We could get halfway to town by then. Maybe even closer.

Besides, my friend was out there. We'd had a fight, that was true. But maybe Frank was right. Maybe I was just a stupid city kid. Maybe the choice to walk was a good one.

I wanted to catch up with Frank, but he didn't make it easy. He was just a dot against the snow when I left. And he was still a dot up ahead of me. A little bigger, but still just a dot.

Why doesn't he take a break? I asked myself. *Why doesn't he look back and see me?*

Why should he? came my other voice.

It's not a good thing to start talking to yourself. It's a sure sign that you're losing it. Losing your grip on things. But maybe I had good reasons. Two freezing days out on the land. No food in two days. No real water, just ice and snow melted in my mouth. No real heat. Nothing but a warm snowmobile . . . and now we didn't have that.

So I kept on walking. I was gaining on Frank, just

a little. He had maybe a half hour head start. Now I was maybe twenty minutes behind him. If he'd just turn around. . . .

Frank must have reached the river. He seemed to change direction up ahead. Then he seemed to stop. I was almost ready to shout at him, but I knew he was too far. Instead I walked faster. I could see him clearly now, up ahead. He must be taking some kind of break. Or maybe. . . .

I heard something. I pulled back the hood on my parka and listened. It was an engine. In a second, I could see it. In the distance was a small plane.

"Hey! I shouted. I knew that nobody could hear, but I shouted. "Hey, down here."

I jumped up and started waving like crazy. Then I ran in a big circle, waving. *Leave a mark on the snow,* I told myself.

Frank was doing the same thing. I could see him, waving at the plane.

It was a small plane. Not like the first day, this was a small plane. Maybe a rescue plane. It wasn't right over our heads, but off to one side. How far away was it? Five miles? Ten miles? I had no way of telling.

Could the pilot see us? Could anybody see us?

Then I heard something else. A shot. I turned and saw that Frank had taken out his gun. He fired another shot. There was the clap of the shot, and a puff of smoke.

He wasn't shooting at the plane, was he? I asked myself. *No, he's just making noise. And why not? We had nothing else.*

I looked back up at the plane. It seemed to tip its wings. Was that a sign? Did that mean they saw us?

No, it began flying away.

But still, somebody was looking. That was a search and rescue plane. I was sure of it. It must be flying a grid, looking for us. It had come close. Surely it would be back. Surely it would get closer and see us.

I turned to look at Frank. I knew he must have seen me. I was going to wave and signal that he should hold up. He should wait for me.

But when I looked toward Frank, I only saw part of him. I only saw his coat and hood, not his snow pants or his feet.

That could only mean one thing.

And it was the worst thing.

Chapter 10

The Worst Thing

So I ran. I ran as fast as I could in snow pants, my boots sinking into the soft snow left by the blizzard.

It took me maybe five minutes to reach Frank. But that was five minutes too long.

Frank had fallen right into the river. He'd broken through the snow and crust of ice. Now half of him was down in the frozen water. He was holding himself up with his arms, but he couldn't pull himself out.

"Ray, I think I messed up," he said.

Frank wasn't scared. He wasn't angry. He was just himself – honest, kind of funny.

"I should have come with you," I told him. "Let me get you out of there."

Frank's face was white. He hardly seemed to be breathing.

"You gotta be careful, buddy," he said. "Did I ever tell you how ice breaks up in the spring? One day it's solid ice. Next day, you break right through."

"Yeah, you told me."

"A little fresh snow, and you can't see nothin'."

I lay down on the snow and edged toward him. I had to be careful not to put too much weight on the snow. If I did, the ice could crack again . . . and then I'd be in the water.

I moved forward like a crab. "Grab my hand," I said.

"There's no point, Ray. I'm done. It's all over."

"It's not over . . . grab my hand. I'll pull you. You push out with your other hand."

"I can't do it," he said. His voice was very weak. "The water . . . the water's so cold. . . ."

"Frank, just hang on," I told him. "I'll grab your hand and pull you out."

He didn't answer at first. I moved forward a little. I could just about reach his right hand.

"You're crazy, buddy. You're gonna kill yourself . . . get back . . . get away. . . ."

"Frank!" I screamed.

But he pulled his hand away. I was reaching out for him, ready to take hold, but he pulled his hand away. Then he looked at me. There was a look in his eyes. A terrible look. He'd made up his mind.

"Go . . . live . . .." he whispered.

He took his other hand off the ice. Then he started sinking.

"Frank, don't. . . ."

I never finished the words. I wanted to say *don't give up*. I wanted to say, *fight just a little bit more*. But it was too late.

He was gone.

• • •

I don't know how long I lay on the snow. I don't know how I pulled myself away from the hole in the ice and snow. I don't know how I found the will to live. Maybe it was in Frank's final words: go, live. That's what he wanted me to do. If I could. If I could find a way.

Go back to the cave, I told myself. *Find the cave so you can survive one more night.*

Good thinking, I said to the voice.

Go. Go to the cave. Stay alive.

But where was the cave? I had been following Frank to the river. Which direction had I come? The wind had blown snow over my footprints. How could I find my way back?

Stop and think, I told myself. *Look for the sun.*

I had no compass, but I did have the sun. Where were the shadows? I tried to remember, then tried to remember where I walked. The shadow would fall toward the south. But I hadn't walked exactly south. More southwest.

To get back to the cave, I had to walk northeast. How far? Maybe half an hour.

I got to my feet and looked at the shadow. Then I marked the snow. I turned and walked away from my mark. I was only a few minutes out when I turned back to look. The river was frozen over again. There was nothing to mark where Frank had died.

No, that's not true, I told myself. *You left the Ski-doo's snow flap.*

Yeah, I might need that, I answered.

Keep going, a voice said. *You'll survive this.*

What voice was that? I wondered. It wasn't a good sign that I was talking to myself. I was starting to lose it, just like Frank.

Focus your mind, said the voice.

Who's that? I asked.

The voice didn't answer. I looked at my watch – noon. Another six hours of light left. Maybe the plane saw us. Maybe the plane would send help.

But twenty minutes later, I knew I was in trouble. I should have reached the cave. I should have seen the snowmobile. But I saw nothing. I might even have walked right past them.

And now I was lost.

What now? I asked myself.

Circle back, a little north, said the voice.

So I did that. But by one o'clock I was still lost. Everything was white. Everything was the same.

It was cold. So cold I couldn't feel it anymore. I just felt tired. I wanted to lie down and rest. I wanted to give up the struggle.

I was ready to die.

Why keep fighting? I asked myself. *You're out here alone. In the Arctic, freezing, all by yourself. Your best buddy is dead. And maybe you should be dead too.*

Stop it. That was another voice in my head. *Things are bad, but they're not over. It's not over until the fat lady sings.*

My dad used to say that. It's not over until the fat lady sings. What did that mean? Who was the fat lady? Why didn't I ever ask him that?

But maybe when I die, maybe then I can ask him. Some people think so. Maybe there is a heaven and maybe I'll get there. I just have to let myself go. . . .

Up ahead, up against the snow, I saw a white shape. Maybe it was snow blowing in the wind. Maybe it was a cloud low in the sky. Maybe it was death itself.

I fell to my knees. I was ready.

Chapter 11

Where's Your Buddy?

The white shape was the snow plume from two snowmobiles. The plane had seen me. Search and rescue had sent help.

I heard the men before I could really see them. And even then, I couldn't believe it.

It's here, I told myself. *The rescue is here.*

I told you, said the voice.

I was on my feet when the snowmobiles got closer. I found enough strength to wave.

"I'm here!" I shouted, though I knew they couldn't hear.

In two minutes, the men had stopped on both sides of me. The snowmobile engines still growled as

one guy came up to me.

"Ray Macklin?" the guy said.

"Yeah," I replied.

"Where's your buddy Frank?"

And that's when I lost it. I started crying and wailing like a child. I fell to my knees again. I couldn't talk. I couldn't stop the tears. I still can't stop the tears.

· · ·

Do people blame me? No. They say search and rescue was too slow. They say we just had some bad luck. They think we were just two teenagers who did something stupid. We went out on the land before a storm. We didn't tell anybody. We didn't bring what we needed. A lot of people say it's a miracle we lasted so long.

So long. But not long enough.

But I still ask the question, is there something else I could have done? If I had gone with Frank. . . . If I could have made him stop. . . .

There are so many other "ifs." If the snowmobile had started up. . . . If we'd had even a little food. . . . If search and rescue had found us earlier. . . .

My mind has gone through every "if" there is. It doesn't help, of course. I see a doctor now to talk about it, so I know it doesn't help. Frank's gone. That's the simple truth. I have to learn to live with it. I have to keep on with my own life.

Because that's what he said at the end. "Go . . . live. . . ."

So I'm trying.

Hostage

by ALEX KROPP

Rob was just making a bank deposit when the robbers burst in. Soon he's one of six hostages down on the floor, trying to keep the trigger-happy bank robbers from losing control. At the end, Rob is the only hostage left – his life hanging by a thread.

Lost

by SHARON JENNINGS

Rafe Reynolds thought it would be easy to lead a group of kids into wilderness camping. But soon he's lost in the woods with one of the campers. Together they have to deal with everything from bears and broken bones to anger and fist fights.

Overboard

by E.L. THOMAS

An accident at sea leaves Tanner in a lifeboat with his kid sister and a guy he really despises. The survival of the group depends on their working together. But as the hot sun beats down and the water runs out, their chances don't look good.

Wave

by D.M. OUELLET

Luke and Mai could see the tsunami coming at them, but that didn't give them enough time to get away. When the wave hit, they fought to breathe and fought to reach dry land. And that was only the beginning of the disaster.

Quake

by ALEX KROPP

When the first earthquake hits, Cyrus is still at home. He leads his sister to safety, then heads to the local hospital to help other victims. That's when the aftershock hits – the second quake that buries him alive.

Lori Jamison is the author of *Running for Dave* (HIP Sr.) and *Choose Your Bully* (HIP Jr.), as well as all the teacher's guides for HIP novels. Lori is best known as a literacy expert who has written seven professional books for teachers. She speaks at conferences and teacher meetings across North America on issues related to reading and writing development.

For more information on HIP novels:

High Interest Publishing
www.hip-books.com